A NURSE GOT ME

ZOE

JUST BAE

CONTENTS

CHAPTER ONE

At 1600, the alarm on Zoe's phone started to buzz and jingle, ending the nap that would carry her through the first night of three in a row. Zoe stretched out on her soft feather bed, fingertips grazing the touch screen and silencing the annoying alert while a lazy yawn. Wiping the sleep from her eyes, she swung her bare legs over the edge of the mattress. Zoe rolled and shrugged her slender shoulders, sitting on the side of the bed and sliding the weight of her cozy down comforter from her lithe frame. With a natural and unpracticed grace, she treaded softly into the master bath. Going back to work after being off for a stretch was always so bittersweet, she reveled in her time off but always looked forward to catching up on the latest with her friends at work. Silver Bay General

Hospital was like an information superhighway, always drama. While Zoe did not partake in gossip, she was not above listening to it… she was human after all.

'Oh!' Zoe blurted, glancing in the mirror briefly before the steam from the shower began to cloud the glass. Despite her days off and the sleep she thought she had caught up on, she still spotted to her disappointment the slightest trace of darkness under her blue eyes. The nightshift was taking its toll but she absolutely adored the nurses and patient care techs on the overnight. For the past 6 years, Zoe gave her life as an RN in the Surgical/Trauma Intensive Care Unit at SBGH. Of the four critical care areas, the SICU was by far the largest. Ever since graduating from nursing school, Zoe knew she wanted to be where the action was. As a new grad, Zoe knew she'd start in a medical-surgical unit, where she would hone her nursing skills and work her way into the trauma unit. Though Zoe craved the adrenaline, she stayed at bay as a staff nurse in tertiary care until a dreaded meeting with her old supervisor, Nurse Herron.

Nurse Herron was a battle-ax, plain and simple. The younger nurses in the unit called her 'old school', because of her stark white uniform with the nurse cap that looked as though it belonged in the

Smithsonian rather than the modern world. The uniform never displayed a wrinkle and Herron wore it proudly. "Zoe, dear… you are ready." Zoe smiled, stealing herself back to the present while idly washing with a pink loofah that was foaming her favorite lemon and lavender Bath & Body Works soap. After toweling off, she slipped on a white cotton sports bra and matching bikini before dressing in her 'hospital blues'. The ciel-blue scrubs were provided by the hospital for certain units only, which included the ICUs and the OR… areas that were most contaminated. While they didn't have the most flattering appearance, they were laundered and sterilized daily.

Not one to wear makeup at work, Zoe gently sponged on a touch of concealer and coated her long lashes with mascara. With precision, she finished off her look with her favorite lip balm and pressed her lips firmly together. It was unusually warm out for October and Zoe opted out of blow-drying her long, damp copper tresses. After a quick comb through, she wove the strands into a low fishtail braid which she draped over her shoulder after securing the ends with an elastic band. As she tucked a few loose pieces behind her ear, her gaze dropped to her phone which buzzed on the sink.

"Hey, girl. It's my turn to stop at Starbucks. Venti Pumpkin Spice again?"

Zoe's lips curled into a small lopsided grin as her slender digits typed effortlessly across the screen, sending the thumbs up emoji back to her best friend and coworker Amber. Almost instantly, another text buzzed in.

"Don't forget, it's Halloween… and as if the gods wanted to punish us further, the moon is full. It's going to be an absolute nightmare. I hope you packed your big-girl panties."

"Fuck."

In the past 6 years, Zoe had never sworn so much in her life, it surprised even herself at times as she punctuated her vernacular with cuss words. Frequent exposure to trauma changes people and she was no different, experiencing tragedies more so than miracles. They say "Silver Bay is a dangerous place", this fact only made more evident by the hospital capacity being at or exceeding a hundred percent, always. Her eyes narrowed as she stared at the date on the screen, *October 31st… Halloween. Amber was right.* Peeping again, Zoe nodded to her reflection and popped the phone into her front-chest pocket.

Always prepared, dinner was already packed in her lunch bag and waiting on the top shelf of her fridge. Next to it, a large therm0 of cold water. Zoe grabbed both and tucked them into a large-flowered tote that she used only for work and zipped it up, scanning the kitchen for any other items that may have strayed. A creature of habit, Zoe flipped on the light over the kitchen sink and activated the alarm panel, securing the two-bedroom townhouse and snapping up her keys on her way out the door. After locking the deadbolt from the outside, she kneeled down on her small stoop next to the stairs where her jack-o-lantern sat. Using the stem, Zoe gingerly removed the top and turned on the LED light inside which illuminated the pumpkin face. 'Carving pumpkins is not my forte' she said to herself, replacing the lid and skipping down the steps to head towards her white GMC Yukon.

Honestly, the Yukon was too big for her. However, once Zoe had started in the medical field, her father Lou Walker, had insisted she buy a vehicle that was not only safe but would be reliable in all types of weather. Being considered essential personnel meant that reporting to work was not optional, even in times of crisis. The dead could walk the earth and the medical staff would still be expected for assuming shift. The Yukon would easily sweep the dead from the streets Zoe thought, chuckling to herself. Still, the truck was huge for a single woman, but comfortable.

———

Zoe hardly hit traffic working on the off-shift, heading in and out of the heart of Silver Bay opposite of the commuting flow. The Yukon rolled into the parking complex and followed the ramps to the roof, where employees parked. Typically, Zoe tried parking in the same spot, next to the elevator and under the halo of a garage light. As hoped, her spot was open and beside it, a shiny silver BMW x5 idled quietly Amber's SUV. Amber waved, grinning and waving a coffee in each hand; her light brown curls were pulled up into a messy bun atop her head, gently bouncing with her giddiness. 'Well, she seems to be well-caffeinated already.'

With both engines off, Zoe and Amber climbed from their seats and met at the elevator.

"Here you go." Amber handed the piping hot cup to Zoe.

"Oh, thank you! What—"

Zoe had pressed the button for the elevator and was abruptly interrupted when the familiar sound of sirens screamed. The two young nurses looked at each other, eyebrows raising. 'It's already begun.' As the sirens grew closer, Zoe and Amber stepped to the edge of the garage, ignoring the arriving elevator. A med-flight ambulance was speeding towards the ER, close behind a parade of Silver Bay police cruisers followed, their blue lights flashing and strobing in sync with the ambulances red ones. Without looking away, Zoe asked, "What do you think it is?"

CHAPTER TWO

Before appearing on the unit, Zoe and Amber ducked into the ladies locker room to switch into their work clogs. When the pair arrived in the SICU, their nurse supervisor, Katharine was conducting an impromptu staff meeting. Katharine was a woman in her own category, much like her previous manager Nurse Herron, but more fearless. She was her staff's most supportive champion, always doing right by her nurses. She handled conflict with poise but wasn't certainly one to cross, especially if you were a surgeon abusing power in her unit. Physically, she was even more imposing, the statuesque blond woman was stacked in all the right places. She kept her icy blonde tresses short in a no-nonsense style, accented by tailored pants suits… never wearing a skirt. Angular features and high cheekbones combined with her frame gave Katharine a fierce high-fashion, editorial look, striking without any cosmetic influence. As if she wasn't perfect enough, Katharine was also very skilled in critical care and thought nothing of changing into scrubs and helping out on the unit, working alongside her staff.

Zoe felt fortunate, as she watched her leader command the attention of the room. She had been 'groomed' into the nurse she was today by Herron and Katharine. When Zoe was deemed 'ready' by nurse Herron, Zoe left her old unit as a one who was bright, motivated, and easy to teach. However, despite Zoe's maturity for twenty-six, she was shy and meek, one could even argue she was a pushover and easy to manipulate. In six years, with the aid of Katharine and the SICUs seasoned nurses, Zoe began to develop confidence and wielded it effortlessly in simple and complex situations alike. With patient care always at the forefront, Zoe earned the respect of both her peers and surgeons. 'Zoe, focus', she told herself. It was then she saw Katharine holding up a bright red pager, 'the trauma beeper.'

"Alright everyone, as we all know… it's Halloween." Katharine's confident voice paused and nurses and care techs nodded, whispering among themselves. "I have brought in extra staff to assist us with the expected onslaught that we will probably come in. Per the hospital board, all staff who are in direct patient care over the next week and picks up overtime will be given bonuses at the end of next month." There was a soft chatter of excitement, however, the veteran staff looked at one another worried. The hospital was not feeling generous; they expected complete and utter chaos.

Almost as if it were timed, there was a sudden deafening thunder. Everyone fell silent, eyes wide and shining. The only sounds heard were the soft beeps of monitors, medication pumps, ventilators, and life-support machines. Katharine swiftly sidestepped to the charge nurse station's computer and brought up the hospital's news feed. Everyone followed quickly behind her.

"BREAKING NEWS" flashed across the monitor and everyone gathered. There was live footage of an industrial area of Silver Bay, where warehouses, factories, and mills littered the seaport and its scattered piers… completely engulfed in flames, whipping and licking the air, consuming everything in its wake. Zoe's mouth gaped open and she looked over at Amber, who was gasping in disbelief. The SICU staff was completely floored, the silence finally breaking as a pretty brunette by the name of Josie spoke up. "We are going to have a lot of burns to manage tonight. Get ready."

Katharine shook her head slowly, face remaining glued still stuck on the screen. In a voice that seemed far away, paling in comparison to her demeanor just moments before. "No…" Adding even more quietly, "We won't. Fires like that take everything with it."

The realization washed across the group; everyone in that area would likely be burned alive. Zoe felt her mouth go dry as her skin began to prickle. She tried unsuccessfully to swallow her stomach back down from her throat, soft fingertips brushing and covering her lips. She felt Amber rest her head softly on her shoulder, the fingers of her free hand intertwining with that of her friend's.

Suddenly, the phone rang and the trauma beeper screeched to life. Some jumped while others remained lost still in thought. Josie answered the phone. "Hello? Yes. Understood. OR Seven with ETA of four hours. Multi-trauma. K9 Police officer… wait, what do you mean the dog won't leave?" Josie raised her eyebrows as Zoe watched her furiously scribbling down details of the incoming admission.

Josie continued, "This is ICU. We can handle it. What? What do you mean they're staying down here?

We are barely going to have enough room to accommodate patients let alone a troop of cops and a dog!"

Katharine snatched the phone from an exasperated Josie and simply said, "Bring the damn dog."

Katharine hung up the phone and glanced at Josie, while she understood the plea of her trusted head nurse, arguing with the admissions department, it would get them nowhere. Josie quickly regained her composure, passing out the assignment for the night. Non-critical patients had been moved out of the SICU in preparation for things to come, so there were a lot of empty rooms. They would fill quickly tonight and everyone standing there now, would be a different person come the morning. Josie swept a dark curl from her forehead with the back of her hand while dark chocolate eyes lifted under a thick curtain of ebony lashes, fixating on Zoe and watching her thoughtfully.

"Hey Red?" Zoe immediately lifted her stare to meet Josie's. "This one is yours. A decorated K9 police officer with multi-trauma, ETA is four hours. The dog is with him; a black Rhodesian Ridgeback by the name of Rudy. There'll be a large police presence for his and our protection."

Zoe nodded, making mental note of the details as they spilled from the lips of her head nurse. "Amber will be your secondary, it sounds like you will need it. I will call respiratory for a ventilator, touch base with pharmacy… your big boy is over 6'6 and his weight-based meds will require additional concentration to keep him sedated and comfortable. Additionally, you'll need a bed extender."

Compliantly, Zoe nodded again, it would be a lie if she tried to deny her apprehension but this was her purpose. Amber was already on the phone with supply, looking for a bed extender while the other nurses scattered to their rooms to begin their shifts. Katharine who had suddenly disappeared, reappeared dressed in scrubs. She looked apprehensively at Josie, who was juggling between the phone and the pager. They exchanged worried, close-lipped smiles and nodded to one another.

The pager screamed, again and again, everything was coming to life and the unit bustled with activity. Like a well-oiled machine, the staff worked with a fervor, anticipating the needs of what the shift would bring. Silver Bay tonight would have their hands full.

CHAPTER THREE

The SICU was the largest ICU in Silver Bay General Hospital and was also the most recent to get renovated. The twenty-four room section was modernized with the latest technology. The shift had only been a few hours in and the 24-bed unit was nearly full. Besides, there had been 3 codes so far, one of which where the patient survived. Zoe watched as two morgue carts wheeled past her assigned room while she and Amber continued setting up. Room 24 was quite big at the end of the hall. Getting the report of the patient and list of several officers and a dog arriving, Zoe, in fact, hoped it would be large enough. Slowly, she turned to watch Amber who was setting up some suction canisters. "Hey!"

"Hmm?" Amber turned and eyed her friend who

had paused. Zoe took her to the open glass slider and pulled back the privacy curtain. They were almost toe to toe, when Zoe inched close to Amber's ear, whispering.

"Don't you think it's strange. It's Halloween. In past years, we've seen first-hand rival gangs in Cyprus Row come in here in the dozens."

"So?"

"So… Cyprus Row is such a dump. Anyway, I was thinking about the explosion we saw earlier by the seaport. I wonder if it was caused by fireworks or a terrorist attack."

Amber was nodding as she listened, almost thinking Zoe was going mad. "Girl, if you don't stop thinking about that. We already had 9-11. We don't need another one. Girl, we got work to do."

"I don't know just seems weird." Zoe licked her lips and took a deep breath. "The ambulance we saw when we were coming in was driving from that aread… then, within a half-hour, the entire area is gone, Amber. We might be under attack."

"Does seem a bit odd since you put it that way but don't worry. We'll make it."

Zoe opened the curtain, glancing out to the rest of the unit. In the far corner, one of the patient care techs, Shauna was having a very deep discussion with

Dr. Eric Salinger, a 4th-year surgical resident. To say that Zoe disliked the pair would be an understatement. Shauna was a petite hottie, with mousy fair ash brown hair that was always halfway pulled up. She was ok but not stunning. Zoe always saw her look as though she had taken a huge bite out of a shit-sandwich. Shauna did not get along well with the others either, her poor work ethic and attitude towards everyone including the patients made her an unpopular choice when the nurses needed assistance. The fact that she kept company with Eric did not bode well either. Zoe crinkled her nose as Amber peeked over her shoulder. "Speaking of weird. Look at those two," Amber added.

"Right? They give me the creeps, even more so when they are together like this."

Eric looked okay would be handsome if he wasn't always smiling. That constant grin spoke as if he knew the exact date and time in which the world would end. He paraded around the hospital as if he was already a resident physician, being bossy to nurses and others. His behavior knew no bounds. Eric and Katharine had gone a few rounds before after he had been rude to one of her staff. Days later, he offered the nurse an half-hearted apology that was demanded only by his superiors. According to the other surgical residents, Eric was a butcher in the OR. He preferred patients to be under as little anesthesia as possible, arguing that patients had better responses when awake than not. The anesthesia team was not fooled however, openly and abashedly scolding Eric in front of his peers whenever the topic would come up. Recently, the surgeons and anesthesiologists had grown tired of his antics and his OR privileges were temporarily revoked. Eric was ordered to do research until the hospital board of directors stepped in. The nurses were glad he was confined to a desk in the hospital's library. Yet, here he was… talking to Shauna, nearly nose to nose and her giggling indicated there was something going on.

———

The moment was broken as the sound of a bed being wheeled down the main hall was heard; it was moving fast and there was quite a bit of commotion as several voices loudly tried to speak over one another. The bed, with the length extender that Amber had so nicely found, came briskly around the corner. Anesthesia was at the head, one gloved hand pushing as the other squeezed an Ambu bag, providing the intubated patient with oxygen and mechanical breaths, not of the patients own making. On either side of him, two techs kept pace, each one wheeling an IV pole that had several pumps and channels infusing medications. With so many infusions running, the flashing lights on each of the channels reminded Zoe of a Christmas tree. On either side of the bed, two residents and two attending surgeons pushed, remaining was Dr. Lake, who was the director of the SICU… steering at the foot.

A kind and gentle natured man, Katharine and her nurses enjoyed working with Dr. Lake, who despite his advanced age was as sharp as a tack. Patients and their relatives also loved him; his calm and supportive bedside manner was unparalleled. Though he was the director, Dr. Lake was an expert anesthesiologist and intensivist. One week out of the month, he took his turn in the rotation of the SICUs intensivists, to which there were three others, and performed rounds and fulfilled a week-long on-call schedule. His truest passion, besides patient care, was teaching the residents who rotated. Each resident would be completely under Lake's spell as he talked and taught; frequently scribbling notes and answering questions he would quiz them on.

Zoe was relieved when she saw that Lake was on this week. Amber swiftly unhinged the glass as Zoe grasped the foot of the bed, helping guide the heavy bed. At that moment, her eyes went wide as saucers… she was looking at quite possibly the largest man she had ever seen in her life. Unexpectedly, a cold wet nose touched her fingers and she directed her wide-eyed stare to the furry jet-black mass at the foot of the bed. Glassy brown almond-shaped, intelligent eyes watched her intently. His ears triangular and erect, swiveling in response to new noises, taking in rapidly changing surroundings. Besides that, the dog Rudy was perfectly still, like a statue. The behavior from the K9 surprised her, but Zoe didn't really know what to expect. Having never seen a Rhodesian Ridgeback before, she had quickly cruised the internet for a quick reference. Though she had read its physical description, it paled in comparison to the proud looking animal that was laying in front of her. It was large, maybe 80lbs squarely built and well-muscled, despite this… it was not bulky but rather compact, agile-looking.

"Zoe?" Dr. Lake yelled, her head snapping immediately to face him, as the bed was locked into position in Room 24. "Are you taking our friend here?"

"Yes, Doctor."

Anesthesia stopped squeezing the Ambu bag momentarily to connect the ventilator to the patients breathing tube. Other nurses, including Katharine, swarmed into the room, helping to settle the new admission. None of them spoke but went about the task at hand without any direction, like bees in a honeycomb that instinctively knew what must be done. The in-room monitor came alive, displaying numerous numbers and tracings which indicated the man's vital signs. Zoe agreed to take the report from Anesthesia then, satisfied at the moment with his stable condition. Katharine was at the head of the bed, making a list of all the infusions that were running, dose and volume, confirming also that each channel was programmed with the correct documented weight. Amber took note of all of the man's invasive lines. He had a radial arterial line in his right wrist which showed second-by-second blood pressure, in a red waveform displayed on the monitor just under his EKG reading which was green. The man had a triple lumen MAC line above his left collarbone… instead of having peripheral IVs. This special IV was centralized in the patient's body, directing the medication infusions to his heart via his superior vena cava. This particular one had a way of measuring his cardiac output, the yellow waveform on the monitor belonged to this PA line. "Urinary catheter?" Amber chimed out, another nurse answering affirmatively while taking account of the amount of urine in the bag. Josie who appeared opposite of Amber squatted down and called out, "Chest tube to suction!" as a soft bubbling noise is heard.

Amber moved towards the patient's head and was about to document the placement of the breathing tube, when she did a sudden double-take of his face, gasping inaudibly. The left side of his face and neck was a devastating burned and scarred. His mangled skin was a jigsaw as it twists and craters, around his left eye and Amber wondered if the man's vision is intact. At his jaw, the skin here is especially thin and superficial, it wouldn't take much to expose the bone of his mandible. Her assessment continues, finding he is without a left eyebrow and where his ear should be, is a gnarled stump.

Zoe finishes her scribbled report in a shorthand that only she can comprehend and look to her team. The OR techs begin to file out and Anesthesia heads to the desk to write a transfer note. As she passes Lake, he squeezes her shoulder gently. "I'll write you some orders, dear. In the meantime, blood pressure with a MAP >65, heart rate 60-100 and SpO2 should be >96%. They say ventilating him has been problematic... more than likely due to his size. They put him way under. The officer shall rest tonight and tomorrow, we will wean him off slowly."

Silently acknowledging, Zoe steps up to where Amber is and is also taken aback by the sight. However, it was not the scars Zoe noticed first, and not knowing what possessed her at that moment, her fingers grazed the forehead of the sedated officer and softly brushed slickened black strands of hair that stuck to his face away. Turning her hand, so that the underside was against his skin, her knuckle just ghosting over his right, heavy brow and down his defined cheek. His jaw was prominent and masculine, the slight stubble that grew there tickled her skin. Withdrawing her hand, gaze fixated still on his face, Zoe let out a breath she wasn't even aware that she was holding in. She realized then that she was alone with Officer Sam Dalton, the other nurses had left to settle another admit rolling through. Amber went to tend to a phone call at the desk. Rudy softly thumped his tail against the blankets, making his presence known, in case she had forgotten. Zoe hadn't, she was very much aware of all the work that needed to be done."

Zoe purposefully moved quietly to his right side, leaning to whisper in his ear… just enough over the

bubbling chest tube, beeping monitor, click of infu-
sion channels and whirring of the ventilator.

"I'm Zoe—" Drawing a deep breath, "And we will
spend this night and the next, and the one after,
together."

CHAPTER FOUR

Zoe grabbed a basin and supplies, moving with speed, there was much to be done. Once she was satisfied with Officer Dalton's vital signs, initial assessment and confirmation of having back up medication infusions in the waiting, she began peeling back the hospital bedding which was heavy with saturated blood from the OR and tossed them into an open hamper. Her blue eyes assessed the massive man before her, only covered now in a hospital gown which was rumpled and soiled. With towels and bath blankets stacked beside her, Zoe began to unsnap the shoulder of the sleeves… her gloved fingers fumbling, as if she was a first-year CNA again as if she had never given a bed bath before. Biting down on her bottom lip, she whispered to herself, "Get it together, Zoe!"

As Officer Dalton's bare chest came into view, she felt the heat rising to her cheeks, flooding the pale skin there. He was an absolutely beautiful and massive specimen, and though he lay comfortably in this sedated state, his muscled physique remained impressively hard and defined... as if he was carved from stone in the very likeness of a god. His expansive chest, dappled with dark hair rose and fell in compliance with the ventilator. The right side of his thoracic cage suffered some sort of crushing injury, causing several ribs to break, which in turn punctured and downed his right lung. To help with the re-expansion of the lung, a chest tube was placed and bubbled quietly as Zoe stood and admired the handsome man in front of her, almost in a daze. Voices outside her room brought her back, one was Amber, who was arguing with two men, though Zoe did not seem to recognize. "Zoe!" Amber called out.

Zoe turned to look towards the curtain and could see the heels of Amber's clogs as if she was blocking the door.

"There are two very annoying officers here to see your patient. I told them you were busy right now and they would have to wait."

She heard them again teasing Amber, their boots nearing her clogs.

"Annoying but terribly good looking, eh?" One officer said.

Zoe raised her brows and draped a towel over Dalton's chest, his lap still covered by the bottom half of his hospital gown. Making sure he was adequately covered; Zoe scooted to the door and poked her head out the edge of the curtain and over Amber's shoulder.

"For god's sake, there are some good lookin' nurses here!"

Both officers exchanged a grin before looking back at the brunette and redhead before them. The shorter of the two men ran his index finger and thumb along with his dark goatee before offering a sly but sincere smile, almost speaking directly to Amber.

"I'm Officer Adrian Blumenthal… and this here is Officer Hank Lowell." Nodding his head towards the larger man, who like Zoe, was a redhead. Hank's icy blue stare looked then to Zoe, his thumbs resting gently atop the silver buckle of his belt. "How is our boy?"

Zoe slipped out fully from behind the curtain, finding herself under the imposing stare of what she assumed were close friends of Officer Dalton's. With ease, she folded her hands, having had discarded her gloves before coming to the door and looked at them intently, exuding sudden confidence. "Officer Dalton has suffered many injuries and while I cannot give you specifics right now, what I can tell you is that he is resting comfortably. He is on a ventilator. Once I am done with giving him a bath—" Zoe felt the heat on her cheeks flare again. "I'll let both of you come in and see him." The look of relief upon their faces quickly changed to amusement.

"Where do we sign up for baths?"

Zoe and Amber looked at one another and then shook their heads. Amber hid her lips behind her hand, for fear that even the tiniest of giggles would slip out. Seriously, Zoe folded her arms across her chest. "It would be helpful if you two could call Officer Dalton's family and tell them what has happened and that he's here at SBGH."

"Well, to be honest… Sam doesn't really have any family," Officer Adrian explained.

"How about a wife?" Zoe added. Another soft blush betrayed her intent.

"No!" Hank added, eyeing Zoe's cheeks suspiciously before grinning.

"Girlfriend?" The question passed Zoe's lips before she could even catch it.

"No, lucky for you." Adrian chuckled before giving the blushing redhead a wink.

"Oh! You wicked, wicked man!" Amber giggled melodiously, gently swatting at Officer Blumenthal and then at Hank, whose attention had been directed back to the nurses' station. Hank was staring unabashedly at the statuesque Katharine who busied herself with the phone that wouldn't stop ringing. Zoe excused herself and stepped back into her room, hearing Amber wheeling chairs over for Officers Adrian and Hank. As she returned to the bedside, Zoe glanced to the foot of the bed, where Rudy laid. The dog lazily looked back at her, his head resting on his front paws, body, and tail curled into the remaining space. "Good boy."

* * *

While refilling the basin with warm water, Zoe snatched up several washcloths and a bottle of surgical soap and then wheeled everything over via bedside table. Removing the towel from Officer Dalton's chest, she admired his masculine form, only briefly this time and began working. Gently, she washed the ruined left side of his face first, inspecting the twisting mass of scars which appeared old, as they were healed. The mangled flesh shone as the soapy washcloth removed grime and dried blood. There were no facial fractures but there were the beginnings of bruising. She dipped the washcloth again and tended to the right side of his face, handsome and rugged. She noted a small laceration above his thick dark brow and cleaned it with new gauze, dabbing ointment on it after. Taking the flashlight from beside the basin, Zoe tenderly opened each one of his eyes and flashed the light into his pupils. The officer's eyes were dark grey; the color of storm clouds racing over an angry sea. The pupils briskly constricted to the light, which was the reaction Zoe was expecting, thankfully he was not found to have any head injuries. At that moment, Zoe found herself hoping that maybe tomorrow the distant and glassy stare those stormy grey eyes had now would be replaced with vision, seeing her upon his wake. She shook her head then, repeatedly and silently scolding herself with how unprofessional she was being. This was her patient and she was his nurse.

Moving to the head of the bed, another refreshed water basin in the bin, she stood looking down as him and purposefully started pushing his dark black hair back from his forehead. Noting some glass pieces, she double gloved and picked out the larger pieces by hand and then with a small black comb, cleaned out the rest. As she started to lather his hair with shampoo, she imagined how he wears it when at work... or even at home, a smile tugging at the corners of her lips as she pictured him sporting a low ponytail at the nape of his thick neck. Though she did not think of him to rock a man bun, she twisted his freshly clean and damp hair into a bun atop his head so it would not get in the way of lines or equipment. Idly, she wondered then what it would feel like to run her fingers through his hair under different circumstances. 'Oh, my God, just stop,' she pleaded.

Zoe then moved to continue with the bath. With fresh washcloths, she soaped up his shoulders and chest, avoiding the chest-tube dressing in which she would change to her liking afterward. It would be a lie to say Zoe didn't enjoy giving Officer Dalton this bed bath, and though this type of care was something Zoe gave all her patients, she felt guilty about letting her mind wander while Officer Dalton was in such a critical state. Feeling foolish, she took a deep breath as the washcloth ran down his stomach, over each and every individual abdominal, soaking the trail of soft black fuzz that continued reaching his pubic area, disappearing from sight under his gown. 'He's not even flexing… he is just so yummy- Zoe!'

His lower half still needed to be washed and Zoe felt another wave of heat rush to her face and her stomach filling with butterflies? Pursing her lips together, Zoe let her gaze move to his still-covered lap but as her thoughts began to drift, there was a soft knock and Katharine appeared. "I saw that your curtain was still closed, Zoe. I thought perhaps you needed some help." Relief overcame Zoe, while she remained outwardly professional, she was thankful Katharine's assistance would keep her laser-focused. Rudy alerted to the newcomer lifted his head and swiveled his triangular ears. Katharine smiled at the dog who softly thumped his tail a couple times before settling his chin on his paws.

"I figured we could finish the bath and then ask the officers outside how to get my new friend here off the bed, so we can change the sheets."

"Good idea," said Katherine.

Zoe spread a fresh towel over Officer Dalton's lap before pulling the hospital gown completely away. Katharine at the moment did not seem none the wiser, gloving up and taking a washcloth into her fingers, wringing out the excess soapy water. Shifting the towel to expose the officer's thigh, Katharine carefully began to wash his left leg. "What a shame this happened, Officer Blumenthal and Lowell both say adamantly how dedicated of an officer he is. Dependable, honest, strong. How much he loves his K9…"

Katharine studied his face with admiration, and what may have even been a pity. Zoe was standing watching, and Katharine moved to her side to do the other leg. Similar to the injury to the right side of his chest, his femur had been broken and hip dislocated, both re-set and repaired in the OR. While his orthopedic injuries would be painful and likely require physical therapy, but it was his internal injuries that worried Zoe. Officer Dalton suffered a grade IV liver laceration which caused him to lose a lot of blood. He was present with unstable and unpredictable shock-like symptoms. While in the OR, the surgical team transfused him with units of blood, while searching for the source of the bleeding.

As Katharine re-dressed his hip dressing, she eyed Zoe curiously, wondering why she hadn't yet completed urinary catheter care, after seeing the towel still on Officer Dalton's lap. In Zoe's hesitation, Katharine found her answer and she demurely hid the tiniest, innocent smile. Unaware, Zoe put on another pair of gloves on and reached for another washcloth. Not wanting to place herself in a negative light in the presence of her supervisor, Zoe delicately moved the towel and wasn't prepared for what was underneath.

———————

It is said that nurses see more men private parts than

the ladies of the night who reside on the street of silk. Though Zoe had certainly seen her share, Officer Dalton's was truly exceptional. Zoe's gaze widened, with her dry lips parting… she couldn't be sure, but did she just gasped? Doing her best to avoid any eye contact with Katharine, Zoe moved the washcloth to Officer Dalton's impressive manhood. Though not erect, its length was partway down his muscular thighs. However, it was his girth though that started to make Zoe sweat. Her fingertips were unable to touch one another as she wrapped her slender digits around his thick, veined stick. With the most delicate touches, Zoe maneuvered the washcloth around the head and the rubber catheter. 'Your boss is literally standing a few feet away, get it together you creep,' Zoe thought.

Katharine was now placing new heart-monitor leads on Officer Dalton's chest in attempts to move things along, ending Zoe's palpable tension. With luck, they had found an extra-large hospital gown which would accommodate the Officer's hulking frame. Zoe was pleased, Officer Dalton was squeaky clean with new bandages, besides his obvious injuries and breathing tube, he looked okay. Zoe watched the officer as Katharine left to ask Officers Blumenthal and Lowell about Rudy. When she returned, the redhead was swift on her heels whipping the curtain closed behind her. "Move. You are in our way!"

Josie was sassing the two officers at the door, getting them to move as Amber followed inside.

"Ok. See that K9's harness?" The nurses looked over to the counter where Rudy's harness sat and Zoe looked back to Katharine curiously for more direction. "Right now, it is off… meaning Rudy is off-duty. We have to put it back on him."

"That seems easy." Zoe took the black and olive green nylon heavy harness with military-grade buckles and a few Velcro patches. One read: "I am the Rudy". Rudy suddenly sat up from the bed in full attention. His deep brown stare was hyperfocused on Zoe as she approached him with the harness in hand. He was even more impressive from this angle… angular, lean and athletic. The way he sat perfectly still was almost disarming. Carefully, Zoe began slipping the harness over Rudy head and ears, smoothing straps down and around his chest. Rudy was patient as Zoe worked the harness like a rubrics cube. Finally, Rudy was "dressed" and he leaped from the bed with a graceful agility Zoe, nor the other nurses had ever seen from a dog.

"What a good boy," Amber cooed, reaching for him. The dog who just moments ago was lying upon the bed, thumping his tail to the delight of the ladies was in work-mode. Rudy ignored her advances and silently inched to the closed curtain, in the path of the doorway.

The nurses busied themselves helping Zoe roll her patient from one side of the bed to the other so that all of the soiled sheets could be replaced with fresh new ones. Before leaving, they also cleaned the room; the soiled linen went into the hamper, blood was wiped from the floor and bed rails, all unused linen was folded neatly and placed into the cabinets. All evidence of the chaotic scene it had been when Officer Dalton first arrived was now cleared. Zoe thanked her co-workers gratefully and dimmed the recessed lighting which shone over Officer Dalton's resting body. She smiled and washed her hands before stepping to Rudy in the doorway, ruffling his thick fur behind his ears.

"Officer Blumenthal, Officer Lowell… you can come in now."

CHAPTER FIVE

The two officers stepped past Rudy, the dog didn't move or react, even as they scratched his head on their way coming by. They looked serious; Hank with his mouth slightly agape and Adrian with his lips pressed into a hard line. The color drained from their faces as they took in the sight of their fallen comrade, Officer Sam Dalton. Despite his injuries, both men noted how well-kempt and clean Dalton appeared. He was scrubbed pink, his shoulder-length black hair freshly washed and piled onto the top of his head. The laceration above his right eye was bandaged.

Adrian was the first to come to his bedside, extra careful not to kick over the bubbling chest tube chamber on the floor. Hank followed but stood facing

Adrian. Zoe stood quietly at the foot of the bed, allowing them to take in everything. Of the two, Zoe though Hank was more receptive than Officer Blumenthal. Hank's pale icy-blue eyes welled ever so slightly with salted tears... threatening to roll down his cheek if they filled anymore. One of his hands rested on the bedrail while the other one softly grasped Sam's forearm. "We are here for you, brother. Adrian and me, Hank. And Rudy, too." Adrian looked at Hank as he spoke, then back to Sam who looked so tired, he could have been sleeping. Without taking his eyes off him, Adrian finally spoke, "He looks better."

Zoe smiled as Adrian faced her.

"So, you wash all of him? Like, everything?" Like two teenage boys, the two officers began to snicker. Zoe gave them a curt nod before Adrian continued, "Well, he is not going to like that one bit. Could have bought him dinner first before checking out the goods."

Zoe wanted to laugh, but her professionalism overtook her. "Alright, you two rascals, out. I have things to do." Hank and Adrian exchanged grins again.

"Just wanted to brighten the mood, that's all."

The officers left and Zoe whipped the curtain shut and moved to the equipment cart pulling out blood tubes and other phlebotomy pieces. She then took the blood from one of the lines and wistfully examined Officer Dalton's face. "I will happily buy you dinner when you make it out of here if you like." Placing the vials of blood into a bag and disposing of her gloves, Zoe left the room.

———

Adrian and Hank were almost too large for the chairs Amber had given them, but neither cared for their friend was alive. Adrian was not bashful as he watched Amber scurry around the unit, her passion for work, especially on this night, was appealing for the hardworking, blue-collared man. Despite being so busy, Amber was sensitive to Officer Blumenthal's harden stare... men staring at her was not a new thing for the bubbly brunette with bouncing curls. Amber stepped purposefully with an extra swing, her slender hips taunting Adrian as she darted across the unit. Adrian's lips tugged into a slight one-sided smile as his neck craned to examine the way Amber's curved backside looked as she bent over the desk, answering the phone. "Would you look at that?" Hank stopped talking, realizing Adrian hadn't heard literally anything he said. Hank grunted in response, mildly annoyed. "Think I got a chance, buddy?"

"No. The only thing she would ever let a man like you lick would be the bottoms of those purple clogs."

"I would gladly lick those… before I…"

Both officers straightened up and become quiet as Zoe emerged from the room with a biohazard bag tucked up under her arm as she washed her hands.

"One thing I do know, brother… he is going to like that one."

"Agreed. He is so lucky."

Both officers chuckled. Adrian resuming his stalking of Amber as Hank, significantly less obvious, almost shy glanced in the direction of the beautiful blonde, "the leader" of the nurses he assumed.

———

Zoe found an unused portable workstation and unplugged it from the wall and headed towards the nurses' station where Amber was standing. "He staring you know… like you are a delicious meal." Zoe remarked softly, amused.

"Oh darling, I know. I am that delicious." Amber shot a sideways-glance at Zoe and winked. "How long do you think before I have his balls tucked neatly into my back pocket?" Zoe giggled and in unison, the two nurses challenged the officers, with stares of their own. Caught off-guard, Adrian nearly lost his seat in the rolling chair which caused Hank to roar. Zoe and Amber burst into laughter, even Katharine who was passing through with an armful of supplies was harmless by the laugh of Officer Lowell. Her lips pursed and the smile that formed then revealed her, freezing the wide-eyed Hank.

"Zoe!" Josie chided. "Your labs came back and 24's H&H is low. I paged Lake for you." No sooner had Josie ended, the phone rang again and Dr. Lake was on the other end saying he had ordered blood for Officer Dalton and he should be transfused as soon as the units were ready. Taking a moment, Zoe sipped on her cup of coffee and picked up the phone on the first ring when rang again. Hanging up, Zoe put down her cup and headed over to Shauna, who was sitting idly at the desk, playing with her phone.

"Shauna, would you please go to the blood bank and pick up the blood for Room 24,?"

Pretending she hadn't heard the request, Shauna continued typing and even had the nerve to laugh as if she had read something funny. Zoe squinted; Shawna's antics would not be tolerated tonight. The entire staff was so busy, despite how the hours ticked by and here was Shauna, on her ass, taking up space and converting oxygen into carbon dioxide.

"Shauna!" Zoe snapped. Shawna stopped, tucking the phone into her breast pocket. "Yes?" She pretended in a sickeningly sweet voice. Standing, Shauna invaded Zoe's personal space, though she lacked the height to face her nose to nose. Not affected, Zoe stone-walled the mousy girl whose face puckered and soured into a familiar position. "I need you to get blood from the bank for Room 24, for Officer Dalton."

"You think you are so much better than me," Shawna hissed. "It should be me in your shoes, rich little Zoe Walker with the world at her feet. Too bad all of that money can't buy life for you to get a damn boyfriend." Zoe's eyes narrowed into slits which caused Shauna to smile so wide that it reached her eyes.

"Out of the way!" Amber buzzed, barging her way between the two, shouldering Shauna really hard. Embarrassed, Shauna crossed her slender arms across her less than ample chest, storming off.

"I'll get the blood." Amber was already heading

towards the door that would lead her to the main elevators.

———

Zoe was back at Officer Dalton's bedside priming a new line for the blood as Amber appeared with a small cooler of blood. She had heard her coming when Amber teased Adrian and Hank, "Hi fellas", and cooed Rudy, who hadn't moved. Per protocol, both nurses checked the blood to match the units to both the patient and the order Dr. Lake had written. They signed off on the workstation on wheels that Zoe had rolled into the room to document on. Amber watched Zoe hang the blood, then smile at Sam. A romantic at heart, Amber leaned against the wall and cocked her head purposely. "You like him, don't you?" Zoe stood at his side, one of her hands resting softly on his own large hand as she allowed her gaze to sweep once more over him. "Silly, isn't it?" Amber shook her head softly, a soft curly lock of hair escaping her loose messy bun. "No."

"Zoe, don't let anything that useless cunt, Shauna says get to you. You are better than that…" Before she could finish, Zoe interrupted in a way that only a best friend could. "Come stay over; we get off at the same time." Amber's chin nestled on Zoe's shoulder; she hadn't made a sound. "Hmm, since I already packed. I hope you stocked up on Captain Crunch with Crunchberries!" Amber always had a way of twisting a situation, making light in a time of darkness. Zoe stifled a soft laugh before she nodded and peered back at Amber's large brown eyes.

Zoe and Amber worked on transfusing the reminder of the cooler into Officer Dalton, while Zoe diligently documenting in-between. The extra volume helped Zoe lower Officer Dalton's blood pressure and reduce his heart medications. By 2:30 AM, which also was known as dinnertime, Zoe was even able to turn one medication drip completely off. After repositioning Officer Dalton, Zoe and Amber left the room.

Rudy was gone, as was Hank. "Nature calls." Adrian quipped happily as if reading Zoe's and Amber's thoughts. That wasn't the only thing calling, everyone on the unit was starving and the smell of pizza carried through the unit. Katharine appeared wheeling a metal cart stacked with pizza, the box was familiar... "Pepper's Pizzeria" was the local's favorite in Silver

Bay. Suddenly, the salads that Zoe and Amber had prepared no longer seemed appetizing. The nurses and support staff, with the exception of Shauna, gathered around at the nursing station and sat shoulder to shoulder. Zoe and Amber sat next to one another and across the desk from Josie and Katharine. Engrossed in her food, Zoe listened to the chatter of the others. Some discussed their weekend plans while others babbled about their patients and the craziness that had transpired. "We still have five more hours to go!" Everyone moaned.

Zoe turned her attention back to Room 24. Hank was back with Rudy and was filling a bowl full of water for the K9. Rudy refused and went back to his post, which caused Hank to frown. Putting down her crust, Zoe wheeled over in her rolling chair, propelling herself with her long legs. She then undid the buckles to Rudy's harness, allowing the straps to fall as Hank watched. Rudy stepped out and padded to the bowl, lapping up the water with rapidity. Sliding from her seat, Zoe kneeled next to Rudy who saw her after he had his fill. As water dripped from his black muzzle, a large pink tongue lolled out and licked his black-rimmed chops. "Good boy Rudy. You are so cute... Oh, yes you are." Zoe had both hands in his thick fur when Rudy tipped over in a heap, rolling onto his back and exposing his belly. Zoe's laughing attracted Amber from her meal and soon, both girls were on the floor, scratching and fawning over the off-duty officer. Adrian and Hank watched the girls with Rudy. "Some guys just have all the luck," Adrian said playfully. Amber stood then and without a word curled her index finger under the chin of Officer Blumenthal and began scratching his goatee. "Jealous, are we?"

"Very," Adrian answered, his eyes glued to Amber's ass as she tipped his head back effortlessly, staring down at him. A crooked smirk swept across her lips as he shifted uncomfortably in his seat; the crotch of his uniform suddenly forming. Adrian moved his legs so that they were wide enough to be on either side of Amber's, it took every bit of restraint for him not to pull her onto his lap. As a self-proclaimed womanizer, this was new territory for Officer Blumenthal. Adrian wasn't a bad guy, but he was used to the badge-bunnies and one-night stands. Yet, here was Amber... beautiful, confident and commanding, getting the very best of him...publicly. Hank and Zoe watched wide-eyed in complete and utter quietness, even Rudy had stopped his wiggling. Bending at the hip, Amber leaned in placing both of her hands on each side of Adrian's thighs, grasping the chair seat. Fascinated with their closeness, Adrian sucked in a sudden breath as Amber tilted her head forward as if talking to his lap. "Down, boy."

————

Zoe and Amber were already heading back to the desk when Adrian blinked himself back into reality. Hank slapped him on the shoulder. "I think I'm in love," Adrian sighed and sunk deeper in his seat, tugging at his uniform.

Rudy left behind his fellow officers and padded swiftly to his master's hospital bed, leaping effortlessly between Sam's strategically placed feet, both legs elevated on several pillows so that neither heel would touch the bed. Rudy stared intently at Sam as if he was willing him to wake. When that didn't work, Rudy bumped his nose into Sam's knee and again, slightly harder. Nothing. With a snort, Rudy laid back down, curling his body around himself. Though his eyes closed, his ears remained upright, moving slightly when detecting noise.

————

Morning came, and the night staff was completely

exhausted as the day team trickled in one by one. Amber and Zoe waited for their fill-ins, all the while making Hank and Adrian promise to come back tonight. Zoe had explained to them that per Dr. Lake; Sam's vital signs, chest x-ray, and labs looked fine. Zoe explained she would be turning off the paralytic tonight and lifting the sedation for the first time. Both officers were hopeful by the news and promised repeatedly that they would be the ones on duty again tonight. Their morning fill-ins came in the form of Officer Paxton and Officer Ross, both rookies who were cute. Upon seeing Zoe and Amber, both lit up. "Wow…" Jealousy surged instantly through Adrian, giving each rookie and effective slap across the back of the head. "Don't even think about it." He warned. River and Paxton swallowed at one another nervously.

After the report, Zoe went to Officer Dalton's bedside. Rudy opened both eyes and lazily looked at her. The rookies had brought food for Rudy. In a small bowl, meat and chicken captivated Rudy but he looked again at Zoe instead. "I know, boy. It'll be okay… you'll see. Your master will come back. He has to." Rudy coasted out of the bed, not like he had before and stared into the bowl of his favorites. Zoe urged, kneeling beside him and finally, almost begrudging Rudy made work of the bowl. Zoe ran her fingers through his fur as the dog was lonely without his partner. It broke Zoe's heart seeing Rudy appear so lost; he leaned his heavy frame into her side as they sat together on the floor. The Ridgeback was warm, like a little heater and this brought comfort to Zoe who smiled, draping her arm around ot. "Lets' get you dressed for the day." Zoe took the harness and slipped it easily on, buckling each clasp and making sure all the straps were even. As if the harness were magic, Rudy transformed into the dutiful officer at the doorway. Zoe returned to Officer Dalton, and though she knew she shouldn't, she had to graze the backside of her hand down the ruined side of his face. "I will be back tonight, Sam… nothing will keep me away. Until then, rest easy."

Though Officer Paxton and Ross had been warned, they couldn't help but smile like two green boys as Zoe and Amber walked past, arm in arm, their work bags draped over their shoulders. In the locker room, the girls changed. "Zoe, I'm fantasizing about eating Captain Crunch." Zoe laughed as she pulled up her pair of baggy sweatpants.

The girls took the elevator to the top floor of the garage in the chilly autumn morning. "We survived another Halloween." Amber nodded and grinned. Without another word, they climbed into the Yukon and x5 and followed one another to Zoe's house. Though it had a double-car garage, Zoe parked in the driveway. Amber, who had her own garage door opener pulled her smaller SUV inside, knowing they would take the GMC later. Once inside, Zoe deadbolted the door and put her bag down. Amber was already in the kitchen and had made two huge bowls. "Ah, you naughty girl!" Wiggling her finger at Zoe, both girls erupted with laughter as Amber playfully groped the cereal box, dancing around with it as if it were a long-lost lover. "My dream is to be ass-deep in Captain Crunch one day…" Amber took a huge spoonful and shoveled it into her mouth and Zoe gave her a side-eye glance.

"By the looks of things, your other dream is to be ass-deep in Officer Adrian Blumenthal."

It took a good few minutes for both girls to settle in after breaking out into a fit of hysterics, both red-faced with hot flashes on their cheeks.

Even though the spare room was set up as a guest bedroom, Amber and Zoe always slept together in the master suite. It wasn't unusual for Amber to stay, especially when their work schedules coincided so frequently. No matter how old they got, sleepovers never got old… it was a tradition for them, ever since they were best friends in high school. Zoe crawled under her down comforter and rolled onto her side to face Amber, already tucked in and waiting for Zoe. Nervously, Zoe looked to Amber. "What do you think he will be like, Officer Dalton, when he wakes up?"

"I'm not sure, but if he knows what good for him… he better be nice." Amber shook her fist out in front of her and Zoe smiled. "Especially after you took such good care of him."

Zoe was quiet and Amber knew why.

"Zoe, what are you going to do? Amber started rubbing Zoe's arm.

"I don't know…but let's have some fun."

———

On Zoe's next shift, Officer Dalton had woken up and it was at the most untimely moment.

Zoe was bending over to adjust her shoe when she heard a drowsy gruff voice call out, "nice ass." She spun around to see the giant of a man smiling.

"Thank you," she laughed, and when Dalton smiled back, his whole face lit up.

"I'm Sam," he said simply, extending a hand towards her, and when she took it, he kissed her knuckles gently. "You know how you see and hear things around you even though you're not conscious? I've been waiting to say something to you, Zoe. Thank you for everything. I think Rudy and I owe you more than pizza once I get off this bed."

"I think you do." Zoe could swear that her heart skipped a beat.